BARRON'S

Nick the Knight and the dragon!

This book belongs to a
brave knight named

This is a story about
Nick the Knight.
He is the smallest knight
in all the kingdom.
“Hello!”

There are lots of things that **Knights** should be good at, but because Nick is so small, he is **not** very good at any of them.
He isn't very good at **archery**.

His sword is too **big** and too **heavy** for him to lift.

His horse is too **big** for him to ride.

And he isn't very **brave.**
(He's even scared of spiders!)
"Hehe!"
"Aaaahhh! A spider!"

All of the other knights in the kingdom make fun of Nick for being so small and not very brave. They won't even let him join in playing **cabbage football.**

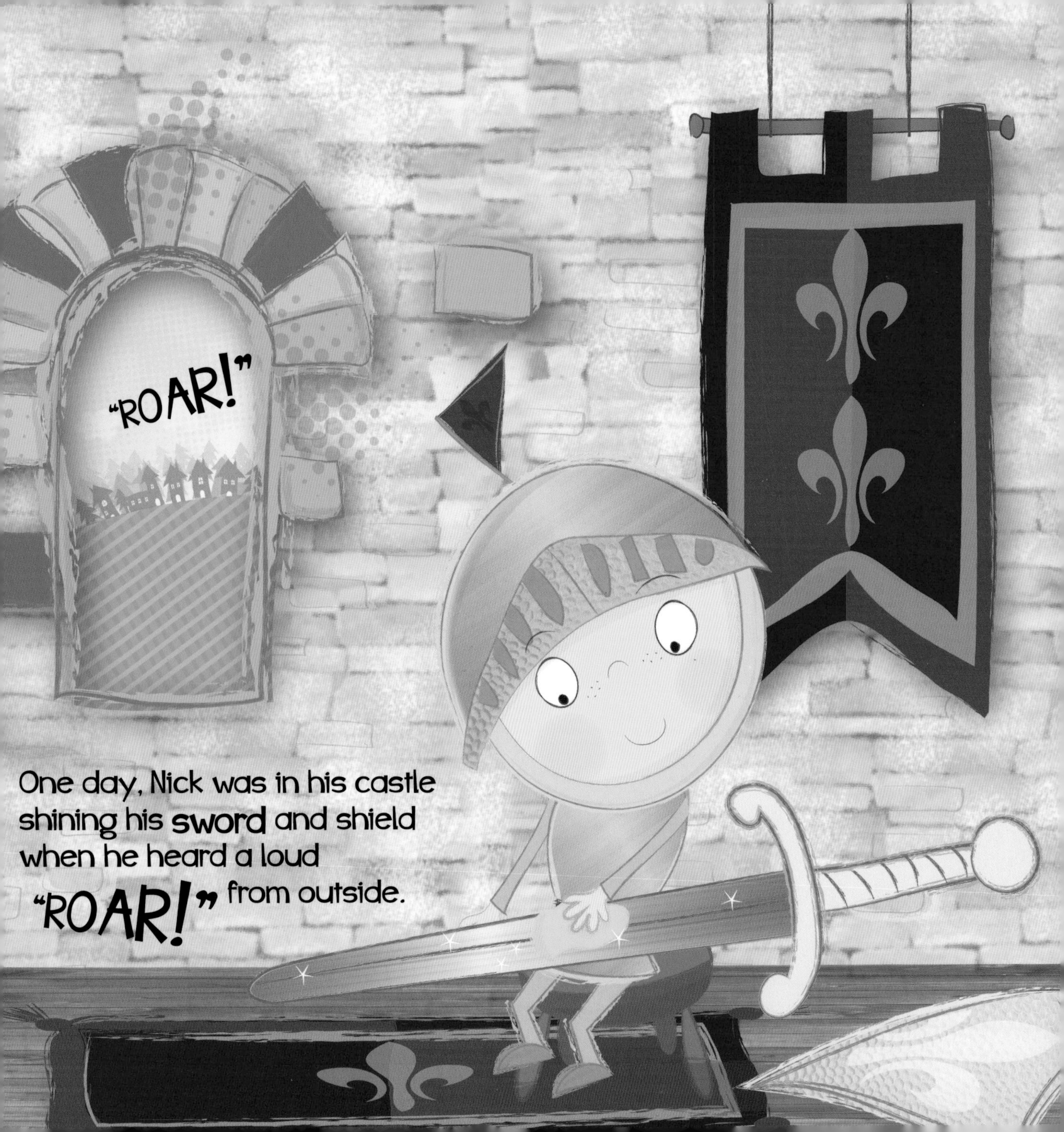

One day, Nick was in his castle shining his **sword** and shield when he heard a loud "ROAR!" from outside.

He quietly tip-toed to the **top** of the castle to see who, or what, had made such a **loud** and **terrifying** noise. As he peeked over the wall, Nick let out a "**gasp!**"

It was the **biggest dragon** he had ever seen!

The **dragon** let out another loud **"ROOAARR!"** and **everybody** in the kingdom ran away as fast as they could.

It was also the **scariest** dragon Nick had ever seen, so he tried to hide behind his shield.

But it was too late.

The **dragon** had seen him . . .

The huge **dragon** flapped its wings and flew over to the castle. It landed next to Nick with a loud **thud.**

The dragon lowered its head next to Nick's and opened its mouth, revealing sharp, pointy teeth and breath that smelled like cabbage! Yuck!
"Oh, no!"
Nick closed his eyes. He was sure he was about to be eaten!

To Nick's surprise, he **hadn't** been eaten!

He slowly opened one eye and peeked between his fingers. The dragon was sitting down and holding its mouth.

"Please, can you help? My tooth hurts!" said the dragon. "Everyone else is too scared to help, and I've got a **toothache!**"

Nick opened his eyes, looked into the **dragon's** mouth, and saw an **arrow** stuck in between two of its **teeth.**

Nick stood up and bravely reached into the scary **dragon's mouth.**
He grabbed hold of the arrow and gave it a **pull** with **all** of his strength.
The arrow came straight out, and Nick fell backward onto the floor with a **bump!**
bump!

The dragon looked at Nick and said . . .

"Thank you, brave knight! My tooth doesn't hurt anymore!"

The dragon stuck out its tongue and gave Nick a **great big lick!**

And with that . . .

the **dragon** wiggled its **tail,**

flapped its **wings,**

and **took off**
into the **sky!**

Everyone in the kingdom soon heard how **brave** Nick had been, and they threw him a big **party** to celebrate . . .

. . . and **Nick** became known as the **bravest** knight in all the kingdom!